This Little Tiger book
belongs to:

For Grandpa Len ~ S S
For Arthur ~ R W

LITTLE TIGER PRESS
1 The Coda Centre
189 Munster Road, London SW6 6AW
www.littletiger.co.uk

First published in Great Britain 2014
This edition published 2014
Text copyright © Steve Smallman 2014
Illustrations copyright © Richard Watson 2014
Steve Smallman and Richard Watson have asserted their rights
to be identified as the author and illustrator of this work
under the Copyright, Designs and Patents Act, 1988
A CIP catalogue record for this book
is available from the British Library
All rights reserved

ISBN 978-1-84895-974-3
Printed in China
LTP/1400/0928/0614
2 4 6 8 10 9 7 5 3 1

BIG BAD OWL

The Daily Grumble

Steve Smallman
Richard Watson

LOOK OUT!
There's a
sheep thief
about...

"Baaaa-humbug"

LITTLE TIGER PRESS
London

It was a dreamy, sunbeamy day
in Cupcake Wood.

Birds sang sweetly. Bunnies hopped
happily. And a big, brown, bumbling bear
was doing what bears do in the woods.

Everyone was happy. Everyone except...

...Scowl.

Scowl was grumpy whatever the weather.

He was even grumpy
in his sleep.

The other animals decided
that **Scowl** needed cheering up.
One little bird had
a great idea.

"You can wear my HAPPY HAT!"
she twittered, plonking it on **Scowl**'s head.

said **Scowl.**

"We just want you to be happy!"
the animals cried. But **Scowl**
didn't give a hoot!

"Twit to you!

And **twit to you too!**" he shouted.

Then he flew off to his
Grumpy Branch
for a bit of peace and quiet.
But when he got there ...

"I AM grumpy!"
screeched the little bird.

"Because YOU broke my
HAPPY HAT!"

Scowl felt funny. For the first time
in his life he'd been out-grumped!
    Red-faced, he flapped off
and rescued the happy hat.
Then he gave it to the
little bird and said . . .

Grumpy

"Does that hat really make you happy?" asked **Scowl**.
"Yes!" twittered the little bird.

Tee hee

Grumpy Branch

"But what makes you happy, **Scowl**?" asked the other animals.
Scowl had a little think. "**Being grumpy!**" he said. "It's **great** fun!"

"Yippedy-doodah!" they all cried.
"So we don't need to do anything
to make you happy?"
    "Well," said S̲c̲o̲w̲l̲, "there is
one thing that you could all do . . ."

And they did.